Goodnight, Magic Moon

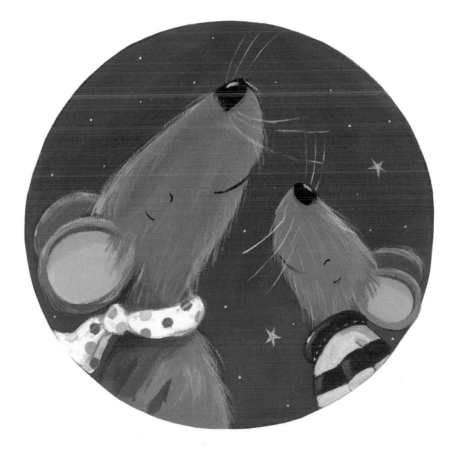

For Heather, with love ~
J.B.
For Linus, with love ~
R.B.

First published in 2009 by Scholastic Children's Books
Euston House, 24 Eversholt Street
London NW1 1DB
a division of Scholastic Ltd
London ~ New York ~ Toronto ~ Sydney ~ Auckland
Mexico City ~ New Delhi ~ Hong Kong

Text copyright © 2009 Janet Bingham
Illustrations copyright © 2009 Rosalind Beardshaw

HB ISBN: 978 1407108 05 6
PB ISBN: 978 1407108 04 9

Goodnight, Magic Moon

Written by
Janet Bingham

Illustrated by
Rosalind Beardshaw

SCHOLASTIC

Nibbles was gathering blackberries in the moonlight. "Catch, Mummy!" he called. Nibbles smiled proudly at his pile of juicy blackberries.

"You've found a lovely, big supper this evening," said Mummy.
"It was easy," replied Nibbles. "It's almost as light as daytime."
"That's because there's a beautiful, round moon tonight!"
said Mummy.

On the next night, Nibbles and Mummy searched for acorns. The night was still bright. But the moon had changed shape. "The moon is shrinking!" gasped Nibbles.

But then Mummy explained that the
Moon Mice had begun their Moon Feast.

"They nibble away at the moon each night
until it's all gone," she said. "And then it grows again,
until it's as round and as bright as before!"

Each evening after that, the moon grew thinner and the sky grew darker. Nibbles found sunflower seeds under the three-quarter moon...

...rosehips under the half-moon...

hazelnuts under the quarter-moon...

and toadstools under the thin curve of the crescent moon.

Then one night, there was no moon at all.
"The moon is all gone!" said Nibbles.
"Don't worry," said Mummy, "the Moon
Mice always leave a tiny edge, too small for
us to see. Then they sprinkle it with stardust,
so the moon can grow again."

It was so dark that Nibbles and Mummy
had to use their noses to find their supper.
Nibbles sniffed the air.

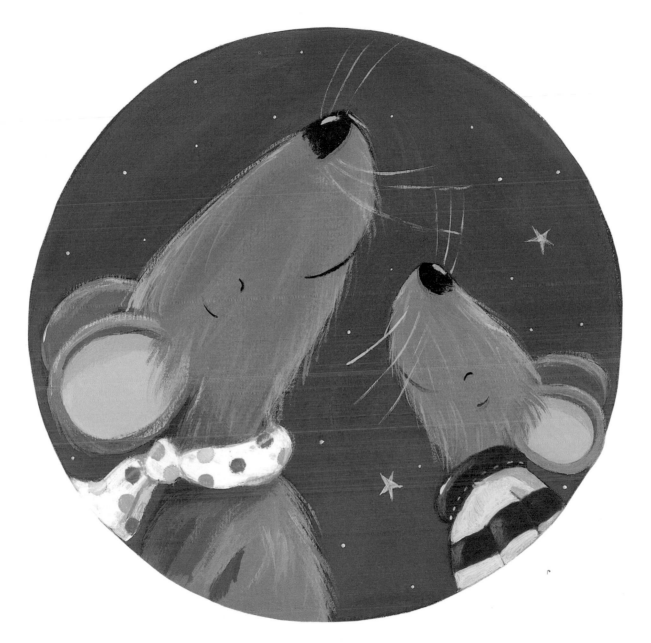

"I smell something," he said, "something very, very nice!"
Mummy and Nibbles followed the
delicious smell across the field.

"It looks like the moon, fallen down
from the sky!" said Nibbles.

"So it does," agreed Mummy. "But it's not the moon. It's a cheese! The biggest, roundest, most moon-like cheese I've ever seen. You *are* clever, Nibbles!"

"We can eat it all up!" giggled Nibbles. "A whole moon-cheese, just for us!"

Just then, a very old mouse came along.
"What a marvellous cheese!" she exclaimed.
"Hello, Mrs Eldermouse," said Mummy.
"Isn't it fine? Nibbles found it!"

Mrs Eldermouse smiled kindly at Nibbles.
"Well done, little mouse," she said.
"I hope you enjoy your special supper!"

Nibbles watched Mrs Eldermouse hobble away. She
looked very tired and hungry. Nibbles looked at
his cheese. He looked back at Mrs Eldermouse.
Then he took a deep breath and called out,
"Would you like some? It's big enough to share."

Mummy broke the cheese up into three pieces and
Nibbles handed Mrs Eldermouse a piece to take home.

"Thank you, Nibbles," she said, taking a bite. "It's delicious!"

Nibbles and Mummy ate their cheese as they walked back to the nest.

"It was very kind of you to share your cheese, Nibbles," said Mummy. "I'm so proud of you.

"And if the Moon Mice were watching, they would be proud of you, too."

Nibbles happily nibbled his cheese until only a thin, curved edge was left. He held it up to the starry sky, and they followed the moon-shape all the way home.

Back at the nest, Nibbles tumbled inside with a yawn.
"Time for bed, Sleepyhead," smiled Mummy.
She tucked him in and began a bedtime story.

"Once there was a mouse," said Mummy,
"who found a round cheese, just like yours.
He was a very good little mouse, just
like you. He shared his cheese with all the
other mice, until only a tiny bit was left..."

"The Moon Mice looked down from the sky and saw what a good mouse he was. So while he slept, they sprinkled stardust on his last little bit of cheese. And when the mouse woke up, that tiny little bit was whole again, as big and round as before, and as magic as the moon!"

Nibbles smiled sleepily.

"I shared too, didn't I?" he said.

"You did," agreed Mummy. "You're a very good little mouse."

"Is my cheese magic like the moon?" asked Nibbles.

"Maybe," smiled Mummy. "Let's hope the Moon Mice are watching. Goodnight, little Nibbles."

"Goodnight, Mummy," said Nibbles.
"And goodnight, Magic Moon." Then, before
he closed his eyes, he put the last little bit of
cheese down carefully beside his bed...

...just in case.